The Chipmunk Song
(Christmas, Don't Be Late)

Christmas, Christmas time is near,
Time for toys and time for cheer.
We've been good, but we can't last.
Hurry, Christmas, hurry fast.
Want a plane that loops the loop;
Me, I want a Hulahoop.
We can hardly stand the wait.
Please, Christmas, don't be late.

A Chipmunk Christmas

adapted by Megan Stine and H. William Stine

drawings by Neil Cole and Corne Cole
color by Cindy Lee

based on a TV special written by
Janice Karman and Ross Bagdasarian

RANDOM HOUSE 🏠 NEW YORK

Copyright © 1985 Bagdasarian Productions. All rights reserved under International and Pan-American Copyright Conventions. Published in the United States by Random House, Inc., New York, and simultaneously in Canada by Random House of Canada Limited, Toronto.

Lyrics from "The Chipmunk Song (Christmas, Don't Be Late)" by Ross Bagdasarian, Sr. Copyright © 1958 Monarch Music Corp. Lyrics from "Dashing Through the Stores" and "Deck the Halls with Smiling Faces" by Janice Karman and Ross Bagdasarian. Copyright © 1981 Karman Ross Music. Reprinted by permission.

Library of Congress Cataloging in Publication Data: Stine, Megan. A Chipmunk Christmas. SUMMARY: Alvin's generous spirit makes a sick child's Christmas very happy. 1. Children's stories, American. [1. Chipmunks—Fiction. 2. Christmas—Fiction] I. Stine, H. William. II. Cole, Corne, ill. III. Karman, Janice. IV. Bagdasarian, Ross. V. Title. PZ7.S86035Ch 1985 [E] 85-1840 ISBN: 0-394-87512-5

Manufactured in the United States of America   1 2 3 4 5 6 7 8 9 0
THE CHIPMUNKS is a trademark of Bagdasarian Productions.

'Twas two days before Christmas and all through the house, not a Chipmunk was stirring—except, of course, for Alvin. He was busy making his Christmas list, and hanging his stocking by the fireplace, and making his Christmas list, and putting signs up on the roof for Santa, and making his Christmas list, and of course there was one other thing he had to do—finish his Christmas list!

When he couldn't think of anything else to ask Santa for, Alvin woke up his brothers.

"Rise and shine, you guys! It's time to go Christmas shopping!" Alvin shouted with glee.

In seconds Theodore and Simon were dressed and sliding down the stairway bannister after Alvin. They screeched to a stop when they got to the living room and saw Alvin's work.

"Is that your Christmas list, Alvin?" asked Theodore. The roll of paper started by the fireplace and went all the way across the room.

"It looks more like an encyclopedia to me," said Simon.

"And why is your stocking so much bigger than ours?" asked Theodore.

"I've been watering it a lot!" Alvin answered. "Come on, you guys. We're wasting valuable shopping time. Let's go wake up Dave!"

Before you could say "Ho, ho, ho," the Chipmunks were in Dave's room, jumping up and down on his bed.

"Hey, fellas, it's six in the morning. The stores don't open for three more hours." Dave groaned as the Chipmunks bounced beside him.

"But Dave, you know it will take three hours to get there," said Simon.

"Yeah—one hour to eat breakfast and two more hours to give us a lecture about never, ever again waking you up at six in the morning!" Alvin added with a laugh.

"Could we make that *two* hours for breakfast and *one* hour for the lecture?" asked Theodore.

"Fellas, I know there are only two more days until Christmas," Dave said. "But I can't go anywhere today. I'm expecting a very important phone call."

"That's okay, Dave. There's only room for three on our skateboard anyway," Alvin said, hopping off the bed. "Come on, guys, let's go!"

"Wait a minute!" Dave called after the Chipmunks. "Don't forget: the Christmas spirit starts at home—not in the store. Be sure to be back by two o'clock so we can decorate the tree."

The Chipmunks zipped off, singing merrily as their skateboard rolled down the sidewalk:

"Dashing through the stores
On a Chipmunk skateboard,
Through the crowds we play,
Shopping all the way!

Stockings hung with care,
Soon Santa will be here.
What fun it is to shop all day
When Dave is nowhere near!"

When the Chipmunks got to the store, it was almost bursting at the seams with people, bright lights, music, and Christmas decorations. They wandered from one department to another and finally wound up in the music department.

"Look, Alvin, there's a harmonica just like yours," said Theodore.

"It's a Golden Echo Harmonica," Alvin said. "The best there is." Alvin took his own harmonica out of his pocket. "But that one isn't just like mine."

"Why not? They look like twins to me," said Simon.

"Because Dave gave this one to me," Alvin said. "That makes it the most special harmonica in the whole world."

Just then a little girl pulled her mother over to look at the harmonica display case. "Look, Mommy, there it is—the Golden Echo Harmonica," she said. "Tommy wants one more than anything."

"I know, Angela, and I wish we could buy it for him," the girl's mother said. "But it's too expensive. We just can't afford it this year."

"Tommy's so sick. I'll bet if he had a harmonica, he'd get better right away," said Angela.

"I don't know what will help, sweetheart," said her mother. "Tommy was very sick for a while, but the doctor says he should be feeling fine by now."

"But he doesn't. Tommy still can't get out of bed."

"I know," Angela's mother said, looking at the Golden Echo Harmonica again. "It's almost as though he doesn't want to get better."

Alvin stood by the display case and watched Angela and her mother walk away.

"Come on, Alvin. It's almost two o'clock," said Simon. "Dave's expecting us back home."

"I'll catch up with you later," said Alvin. "Right now I've got to go see a sick friend."

Alvin ran off to find Angela and her mother. "Angela will be easy to spot," Alvin thought to himself, "because she's wearing a bright red coat."

And it *was* easy to find a little girl in a bright red coat—too easy! The crowded department store was filled with them. Alvin rushed up to one girl after another. But each girl turned out to be someone else.

Finally Alvin gave up and left the store. There was no hope of finding Angela in the crowd. But then a city bus passed by and Alvin's eyes popped open. There was Angela looking sadly out a window!

Alvin hopped on the very next bus and followed the mother and daughter all the way to their little apartment.

He knocked on their door. Angela's mother opened it. "Yes? Can I help you?" she asked.

"Hi. Can I say hello to Tommy for a second?" Alvin asked.

"Who are you?"

"Mommy!" Angela cried behind her mother. "It's Alvin the famous Chipmunk!"

Tommy was lying in his bed with the covers pulled up tight. His face was pale and his eyes drooped.

"Tommy, you have a guest," his mother called to him.

"Who is it, another doctor?" Tommy muttered.

"Nope—it's me, Alvin," Alvin said, approaching Tommy's bed.

"Alvin? From the Chipmunks? Wow!" said Tommy. He sat up with a smile. "I'm your biggest fan!"

"I can't stay long," said Alvin. "I just came over because they had a Christmas contest at the department store . . . in the, uh, music department. And somebody put your name in the big contest hat. And guess what? You won first prize!"

With that, Alvin took his own Golden Echo Harmonica out of his pocket and gave it to Tommy. Tommy's smile took off like a rocket.

"Gee, I'm the luckiest boy in the world," Tommy said.

"Well, gotta go," Alvin said. "Merry Christmas, everybody!"

"It sure will be a Merry Christmas now," Tommy said.

At the front door Angela whispered to Alvin, "We were just in the department store. I didn't see any contest."

"Well, not many people knew about it. In fact, Tommy's was the only name in the hat," said Alvin, giving her a wink before going out the door.

Alvin rode the bus across town with an empty back pocket where his harmonica used to be. But he had a heart full of the joy of Christmas sharing. He got home just in time to put the star on the top of the tree while Simon and Theodore put on strings of lights and popcorn.

"I sure wish you guys had been there to see the look on Tommy's face," Alvin said, telling them his story.

"I can't believe you gave your harmonica away," Theodore said. "I bet Dave's gonna be mad."

"Or his feelings might be hurt because you gave away the harmonica *he* gave you," Simon said.

"But Tommy really needed it," said Alvin. "Anyway, Dave's not going to find out. I'm going to save my money and get another harmonica right after Christmas. He'll never know—and you guys have to promise not to tell him, okay?"

Theodore and Simon looked at each other and then nodded to Alvin.

Just then the telephone rang in the hall.

"I'll answer it," Dave yelled from the closet where the Christmas decorations were kept. "It's probably the important phone call I've been waiting for."

A minute later there was a loud crash.

"You're kidding!" the Chipmunks heard Dave say.

"It *must* be an important phone call," said Simon. "Dave just dropped the box of ornaments he was carrying!"

"Great news, fellas!" Dave said, leaning into the room with his hand over the telephone. "We're going to play Carnegie Hall on Christmas Eve. And the concert is completely sold out."

"Whoopee!" the Chipmunks shouted.

"And they want Alvin to play a harmonica solo," Dave added.

"A *harmonica* solo!" Alvin said, falling off the ladder by the Christmas tree with a crash.

"Alvin's floored by the news!" Dave said, smiling into the telephone. "He can't wait."

"I'll tell you what I can't wait for," Alvin whispered to his brothers. "I can't wait until *after* Christmas to get a new harmonica. I've got to get some money before Christmas—fast!"

Just then Alvin heard some dogs barking next door. He got an idea. "That's it!" he yelled.

An hour later Alvin was in the backyard, dressed in a Santa Claus costume. All the neighborhood dogs were there too. Alvin had dressed them up to look like reindeer.

Simon and Theodore spread the word quickly to all of the kids on the block: Have your picture taken with Santa Claus for only a dollar! It didn't matter that Santa was a little on the skinny side and most of the reindeer had fleas. All the kids lined up with their dollars, and the money started rolling in.

Dave came out of the house. "What's going on here?" he asked Simon. "I'm getting calls from every parent in the neighborhood that their dogs are missing and their kids are late getting home."

"We're helping Alvin make money," said Simon.

"Another one of Alvin's schemes? I should have known," said Dave. He walked to the head of the line. "Alvin—" he started to say. But Alvin interrupted him.

"My name's not Alvin. It's Santa."

"All right, Santa, I'd like to have a word with you and your elves," said Dave.

"Sorry, you'll have to wait in line like everybody else," Alvin said. "Who's next?"

Denise Johnson was next. She wanted a group photo of Santa, the reindeer, her cat, Nibbles, and herself.

But when the reindeer got a look at the cat, they suddenly remembered that they were dogs! They all took off after Nibbles, running over everything and everyone in their way.

At the sight of the dogs rushing toward her, Nibbles twisted away from Denise and ran for her life. Denise ran after her cat. And the other kids chased after the dogs. It took about two seconds for the entire crowd to disappear.

"Hey, wasn't Dave here a minute ago?" asked Alvin, looking around. He and his brothers were standing by themselves in the snow. Suddenly some of the snow started moving. Then a large lump of it stood up.

"Yikes! It's the Abominable Snowman!" Theodore screamed.

"Theodore! Simon! ALVIN!" Dave shouted from underneath the snow.

"It's okay—it's only the Abominable Songwriter!" Alvin said.

Dave dragged Santa and his helpers back into the house. "Now, what's all of this talk about money, fellas?" Dave asked.

"Well, you see, Dave," Theodore began, "Alvin's just got to get some money fast."

"And just why does Alvin need money so badly?" Dave asked.

Theodore tried to think of a good story. "For an operation!" he blurted out.

"Come on, you guys can do better than that," Dave said. "I want the truth. Simon?"

Simon remembered his promise to Alvin. He couldn't tell Dave about the harmonica.

"Well, uh, actually, Dave, Alvin, uh, needs money to buy a, uh . . . a present!" Simon said.

"Well, I can understand that. And who is this present for?" Dave asked Theodore.

"It's for himself," Theodore confessed.

"So that's what the spirit of Christmas means to you, Alvin? Buying presents for yourself?" Dave exclaimed. He sounded angry. "You'd better go up to your room and think about the meaning of Christmas."

All that night Alvin worried about how to get a harmonica in time for the concert the next day. He tossed and turned in his bed and talked in his sleep. "Money . . . I need money," he kept saying. He was having a terrible dream.

In his dream Alvin was standing outside a big building. Suddenly the door opened and a man said, "Well, don't just stand there collecting dust. Come in."

"Oh, no!" Alvin thought in his dream. "That voice—that face—that mustache! It's Clyde Crashcup, the world's worst inventor!"

"Why am I here?" Alvin said to Clyde.

"Dave tells me you've lost the spirit of Christmas, Alvin," Clyde answered.

"But I haven't lost the spirit—"

"Of course you haven't," Clyde said. "How could you lose it? I've only just finished inventing it! I'm calling my invention Santi Claus."

"*Santi* Claus?" Alvin asked with surprise.

"Catchy name, isn't it?" Clyde said. "Yes, Santi Claus. A kind man with a beard and a hat. C'mon, I'll introduce you. *Voilà!*"

And with that, Clyde threw open a door. There sat Abe Lincoln in a sleigh!

"Clyde, you couldn't invent a headache if I gave you twelve loud radios and a jackhammer," Alvin said. "That's not Santa Claus. That's Abe Lincoln!"

"If that isn't Santi Claus, I'll eat that cute, chubby little reindeer," Clyde said. He pointed to an elephant with antlers.

Suddenly the elephant trumpeted loudly as if to say he'd had enough of the silly antlers and even sillier inventors. The elephant picked up Clyde and sent him flying.

"There's nothing like the exhilaration of discovery!" Clyde said as he landed.

Alvin's dream went on and on. "I need money . . . I need money . . . I need money," he said over and over in his sleep.

In the middle of the night Dave looked in on the sleeping Chipmunks. When he heard Alvin talking about money, he just shook his head sadly and walked away.

The next day was Christmas Eve. By the afternoon, Dave was all keyed up about the concert at Carnegie Hall that night. "Hey, where's Alvin?" he asked, suddenly looking around the house.

"Alvin's not here right now," said Theodore.

"Oh, no!" said Dave. His smile melted like a snowflake on a warm plate. "Our Christmas concert at Carnegie Hall is only a few hours away and Alvin disappears! Where did he go?"

But before Theodore or Simon could answer him, the telephone rang.

"Hello," Dave said into the phone.

"Hello, Mr. Seville. You don't know me but I'm Mrs. Waterford, Tommy's mother. Is Alvin there?" she asked.

"No, I'm afraid he's not, Mrs. Waterford," Dave answered.

"When he gets back," said Tommy's mother, "will you please tell him that his harmonica worked wonders for Tommy? He's out of bed and good as new. You should be very proud of Alvin. And Alvin should be feeling very pleased."

At that very moment, however, Alvin was not feeling at all pleased. He was standing in the department store, surrounded by noisy, short-tempered, last-minute shoppers, and staring at the price tag on the Golden Echo Harmonica in the case. Even with the money Theodore and Simon had chipped in, he didn't have enough cash to buy it.

"Who wants to play at Carnegie Hall anyway," Alvin said to himself. "I'd much rather stay home. . . . Oh, who am I kidding? I'd love to play at Carnegie Hall."

"Excuse me, young man, but I need your help," a voice suddenly said.

Alvin turned around and saw a smiling elderly woman standing there. She had soft white hair. Two strands of it kept falling in her face.

"What can *I* do for you?" Alvin asked.

"Well, I'm very lonely and I'm very, very far away from home," the woman said. "I would love to share the holiday spirit and give a nice young man a Christmas present. How would you like a Golden Echo Harmonica?"

For a second Alvin was afraid that he was dreaming again. He slapped his head to make sure his ears were awake. Then he said, "A Golden Echo Harmonica? But you don't even know me."

"But I've been keeping my eye on you, young man. I think you know what the Christmas spirit is all about. That's why I want to give you a present," she said. She handed Alvin a wrapped package.

Alvin unwrapped the paper quickly. Inside, a Golden Echo Harmonica glowed brighter than the brightest Christmas tree. Alvin was overcome with joy. "Thank you," he said, not quite believing his good luck.

"Well, why don't you play me a song?" the woman said, pushing the two strands of hair off her forehead.

Alvin began to play "Silent Night." One by one, all the frantic people in the crowded, noisy store stopped what they were doing and sang along. When the song was over, Alvin looked up and saw Dave, Simon, and Theodore standing in front of him.

"Alvin, I owe you an apology," Dave said. "Theodore and Simon told me everything. That was a wonderful thing you did for Tommy."

"That's okay, Dave," said Alvin, looking around the crowd of people in the store. "But where did that woman go? She just disappeared."

"I don't know who you're talking about, but we'd better disappear too," Simon said.

"Or we'll be late for our concert at Carnegie Hall," Theodore added.

Dave and the Chipmunks ran out of the store and hopped into a horse-drawn cab. As the horse clip-clopped through Central Park, Alvin told the others all about the woman who gave him the harmonica.

"It's what I've said all along, boys. When you give something to the world, the world will give you something wonderful in return," said Dave.

"Great. Then tomorrow I'm giving away all your ugly old neckties, Dave," said Theodore.

"Why would you do that?" Dave asked.

"So that the world will give you some wonderful new ones in return," answered Theodore. "You really need them!"

And they laughed all the way to Carnegie Hall.

The concert that night was a lot like spending Christmas Eve with hundreds of smiling friends. The audience sang carols with the Chipmunks. And, of course, Alvin played a beautiful solo on his beautiful new harmonica.

Then, in the middle of the concert, Alvin looked backstage and saw Tommy Waterford standing there.

"This is the best Christmas ever," Alvin said. He brought Tommy on stage and introduced him to the audience. Tommy played his harmonica while the Chipmunks stood with a cardboard Santa and sang this song:

"Deck the world with smiling faces
  Fa la la la la la la la la
  Bringing joy to sadder places
  Fa la la la la la la la la

Friends and love are what we need
  Fa la la la la la la la la
  But don't forget your gifts for *me*!
  Fa la la la la la la la la."

Much later that night, in a faraway spot at the North Pole, a happy but very tired Santa Claus arrived home. He took off his jacket and sat down in a comfortable chair in front of a warm fire.

"How did your trip go this year, dear?" asked Mrs. Claus.

"Just fine," Santa answered. "Except for one thing. I know I had a Golden Echo Harmonica for a good little chipmunk named Alvin. But when I got to his house late tonight, I couldn't find it in my sack anywhere. I'm afraid he's going to be very disappointed on Christmas morning."

"Oh, I wouldn't worry about it, dear. I'm certain that Alvin got everything he wanted for Christmas," Mrs. Claus said as two strands of soft white hair fell in her face. And she smiled to herself as Santa fell asleep.

The Chipmunk Song
(Christmas, Don't Be Late)

Christmas, Christmas time is near,
Time for toys and time for cheer.
We've been good, but we can't last.
Hurry, Christmas, hurry fast.
Want a plane that loops the loop;
Me, I want a Hulahoop.
We can hardly stand the wait.
Please, Christmas, don't be late.